A Crazy Day at the Critter Café

by Barbara Odanaka

illustrated by Lee White

MARGARET K. MCELDERRY BOOKS
New York London Toronto Sydney

For Paul—B. O.

For Lisa—L. W.

MARGARET K. McELDERRY BOOKS
An imprint of Simon & Schuster Children's Publishing Division
1230 Avenue of the Americas, New York, New York 10020
Text copyright © 2009 by Barbara Odanaka
Illustrations copyright © 2009 by Lee White
All rights reserved, including the right of reproduction in whole or in part in any form.
Book design by Debra Sfetsios
The text for this book is set in Kosmik.
The illustrations for this book are rendered in mixed media.
Manufactured in China
10 9 8 7 6 5 4 3 2 1
Library of Congress Cataloging-in-Publication Data
Odanaka, Barbara.
A crazy day at the Critter Café / Barbara Odanaka ; illustrated by Lee White.—1st ed.
p. cm.
Summary: A quiet morning in a roadside café turns to chaos when a bus breaks down and a menagerie of noisy, rude animals enters, demanding to be fed.
ISBN: 978-1-4169-3914-6 (hardcover)
[1. Animals—Fiction. 2. Restaurants—Fiction. 3. Behavior—Fiction. 4. Humorous stories. 5. Stories in rhyme.] I. White, Lee, 1970– ill. II. Title.
PZ8.3.0275Cri 2009
[E]—dc22
2007030966

IT WAS A QUIET MORNING at the Critter Café.

The cook was dozing in his cheese soufflé.

The waiter was whistling sleepy tunes

when through the door walked **five raccoons.**

"Hey there, waiter.

We need some grub.

Our bus broke down.

We're starving, Bub!"

The waiter jumped up,

menus in hand,

when through the door came
an **elephant band.**

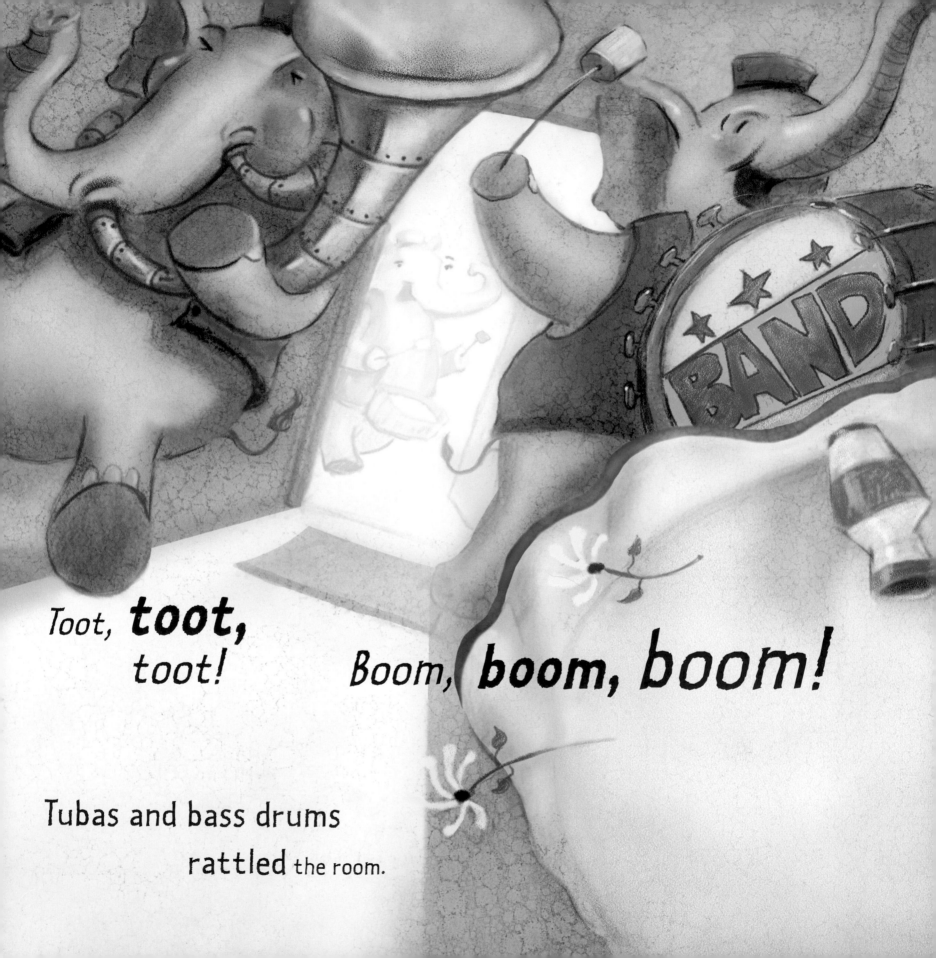

Toot, **toot,** toot!   Boom, **boom, boom!**

Tubas and bass drums
rattled the room.

The raccoons hollered,

"Feed us now!"

when through the door

rolled Skateboard Cow.

Swish,
zoom,
swish.

Clickety-
clack!

Cow spun round,
then **twirled back.**

She was zooming past the apple fritters

when through the door
came a rush of critters.

Macaws, turtles, lizards, lambs,

penguins, zebras, kangaroos, rams . . .

So many creatures poured off the bus,

screeching, squawking—what a fuss!

"Quiet, please,"

the waiter said.

"Just sit down.

We'll get you fed."

Above the din, a wolf pup howled,

"Oh, dear me, my tummy growled!"

And so the orders flooded in:

"Apple pie!" said a pangolin.

An ostrich squawked:

"Cherry strudel!"

"Chips and salsa!" yipped a poodle.

Raccoons crawled
atop their chairs.

Cow skateboarded
down the stairs.
The waiter
scrambled
this way
and that.

"You forgot ME," squeaked a rat.

"**Stop** already!"

the waiter said,

his tray seesawing

above his head.

"Settle down.

Just eat your food.

It might improve your atti—"

"DUDE!"

With tail twitching, Cow zoomed in.

"SHE'S LOST CONTROL!" screamed a pangolin.

Cow lurched this way,
then lurched that,
then crashed into the waiter— SPLAAAAAAT!

The waiter's tray **flipped** through the air, launching food—

E-V-E-R-Y-W-H-E-R-E!

Spaghetti and meatballs, root beer floats,

dropped and plopped on pigs and goats.

Maple syrup, cottage cheese,

splattered chicks and chimpanzees.

A strawberry sundae doused a yak.

A snail flicked kale off his back.

Wiping **cupcake** from his eyes,
covered in ketchup,
milk, and fries,

the waiter staggered
to his knees.
"Achoo!"

Out flew **two buttered peas.**

And don't come back here anymore."

The animals shuffled, shoulders sagging.
Tails tucked, feathers dragging.

"C'mon, critters," their driver said.

"Engine's fixed." And off they sped.

They danced and hugged,
clapped and cheered,
until they spotted
something **WEIRD.**

It looked like a pile of mashed potatoes,

smelled of fish and stewed tomatoes.

It was sleeping soundly—snoring, too—

when it opened its eyes and said,

"Moo?"

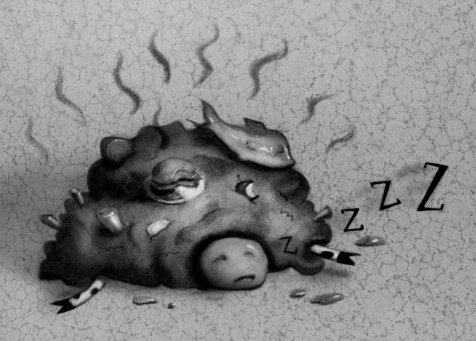

"WOW!" said Cow. "I missed the bus?
And now it's just the *three* of us?
Toss me an apron! Show me the way!

This ol' cow is HERE TO STAY!"

The cook and waiter, too shocked to speak,
shot out the door like a lightning streak.

"But Cook!" called Cow.
"You forgot your hat!"
She tried it on. And *that* . . .